# ERANDI'S BRAIDS

WRITTEN BY Antonio Hernández Madrigal

ILLUSTRATED BY Tomie dePaola

PUFFIN BOOKS

*To my father, Antonio*
*Thank you for the idea*

—A. H. M.

*To Lon Driggers, my American friend in México*

—T. DE P.

## GLOSSARY

| | |
|---|---|
| *buenos días* | good morning |
| *Erandi* | Tarascan female name which means sunrise |
| *fiesta* | party |
| *huaraches* | sandals |
| *huipil* | blouse |
| *Mamá* | Mother |
| *mi hija* | my daughter |
| *Pátzcuaro* | Tarascan village in the state of Michoacán |
| *Señor* | Mr. |
| *Señora* | Mrs. |
| *sí* | yes |
| *tortillas* | thin corn cakes |

PUFFIN BOOKS
Published by the Penguin Group
Penguin Putnam Books for Young Readers, 345 Hudson Street,
New York, New York 10014, U.S.A.
Penguin Books Ltd, 27 Wrights Lane, London W8 5TZ, England
Penguin Books Australia Ltd, Ringwood, Victoria, Australia
Penguin Books Canada Ltd, 10 Alcorn Avenue, Toronto, Ontario, Canada M4V 3B2
Penguin Books (N.Z.) Ltd, 182-190 Wairau Road, Auckland 10, New Zealand
Penguin Books Ltd, Registered Offices: Harmondsworth, Middlesex, England

First published in the United States of America by G. P. Putnam's Sons,
a division of Penguin Putnam Books for Young Readers, 1999
Published by Puffin Books,
a division of Penguin Putnam Books for Young Readers, 2001

10  9  8  7

Text copyright © Antonio Hernández Madrigal, 1999
Illustrations copyright © Tomie dePaola, 1999
All rights reserved

THE LIBRARY OF CONGRESS HAS CATALOGED THE G. P. PUTNAM'S SONS EDITION AS FOLLOWS:
Madrigal, Antonio Hernández. Erandi's braids / Antonio Hernández Madrigal;
pictures by Tomie dePaola.  p.  cm.
Summary: In a poor Mexican village, Erandi surprises her mother by offering to
sell her long, beautiful hair in order to raise enough money to buy a new fishing
net.
[1. Hair—Fiction. 2. Mothers and daughters—Fiction. 3. Mexico—Fiction.]
I. dePaola., Tomie, ill.  II. Title. PZ7.M2657Er 1999 [E]—DC21 97-49631 CIP AC
ISBN 0-399-23212-5

This edition ISBN 0-698-11885-5

Printed in the United States of America
Set in Aurelia

Erandi, it's time to wake up," Mamá whispered. Roosters
were crowing as the orange and crimson colors of dawn
spread across the village of Pátzcuaro, in the hills of México.

Erandi got out of bed, washed her face, and put on her *huipil* and skirt. Then Mamá brushed her hair and wove it into two thick braids that fell to her waist.

When Mamá finished, Erandi helped her prepare the dough for the *tortillas*. As she mixed and patted, Erandi heard voices from a loudspeaker in the street. "Hair! Hair! We will pay the best prices for your hair. Come to Miguel's Barber Shop tomorrow."

"What is that about, Mamá?" Erandi asked.

"It is the hair buyers coming up from the city," Mamá told her.

"Why do they want to buy our hair?" Erandi asked.

"They say it is the longest and most beautiful in México," Mamá explained. "They use it to make fine wigs, eyelashes, and fancy embroidery."

Mamá looked in the old cracked mirror on the adobe wall. Her own hair fell just below her shoulders.

"Your hair is much longer and thicker than mine, Erandi. The hair buyers would pay a fortune for your beautiful braids," she said with pride.

They sat down to eat their meal of beans and *tortillas*. "Do you remember what day tomorrow is, Erandi?"

"*Sí*, Mamá," Erandi said. "My birthday!" She would be seven, and Mamá was going to take her to Señora Andrea's shop to pick out a present. Erandi hoped she would get a new dress to wear to the village fiesta.

They finished eating and got ready to go to the lake. Mamá
packed their fishing net and put it on her back. "Don't forget the
buckets, Erandi," she said, starting off down the trail.

When they arrived at the lake, women and men from the village were already fishing. Erandi's mamá unfolded their net. "Look, Erandi, more holes. I won't be able to repair it any more. We need a new net so badly." Then she paused. "Soon we will have the money to buy one."

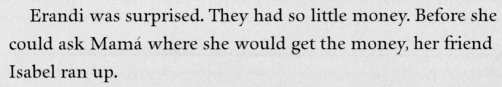

Erandi was surprised. They had so little money. Before she could ask Mamá where she would get the money, her friend Isabel ran up.

"*Buenos días*, Erandi. Can you come and play?" Isabel called.

"Go," Mamá said, "but come back and help me sort the fish."

Isabel and Erandi ran across the fields of flowers. "Are you going to the fiesta next Sunday?" Isabel asked.

The fiesta! Erandi remembered her birthday and the new dress she hoped to wear in the procession. But maybe Mamá needed the money for the new net instead. "I'm not sure," she said.

Throughout the day Erandi went back and forth, playing with Isabel and helping her mamá separate the small fish from the large fish. Then it was time to go. Erandi was afraid to ask about her birthday, and Mamá didn't say anything about it or the new net as they walked home.

But the next morning after making the *tortillas*, Mamá said,
"It's time to go to Señora Andrea's shop, Erandi." Erandi smiled.
She knew she would have a new dress for the fiesta after all.

As they entered the shop in the square, Erandi saw a beautiful
doll wearing a finely embroidered yellow dress up on the shelf.

Mamá saw Erandi stare at the doll.

"Erandi," Mamá said, "what do you want for your birthday?"

Erandi wanted the doll, but she knew she couldn't have both the doll and a dress. She pointed to a yellow dress, the same color as the doll's.

"Maybe next year we can buy you a doll," Mamá said as she paid for the dress.

After they left the shop, Mamá turned to Erandi and said, "Now we will go to the barber shop."

Erandi caught her breath. *My hair! So that is how Mamá is going to get the money for a new net. She is going to sell my braids.* Erandi shivered at the thought of the barber cutting off her braids. But she didn't say anything to Mamá.

They reached Miguel's Barber Shop and went inside. Erandi
looked across the room crowded with women. She gripped
Mamá's hand and huddled in her skirt. She didn't look at the
barber chair, but she couldn't help hearing the sharp *snip snip*
of scissors.

*Will my hair ever grow back?* she worried.

The line of women moved slowly, and Erandi's heart pounded as she and Mamá reached the front.

"Next person!" the barber called out.

Gazing at the enormous scissors in his hand, Erandi felt her knees tremble. But before she could move, Mamá walked to the chair and sat down.

*I should have known Mamá would never sell my hair,* Erandi thought as she watched the barber wrap a white apron around her mamá's shoulders and measure her hair.

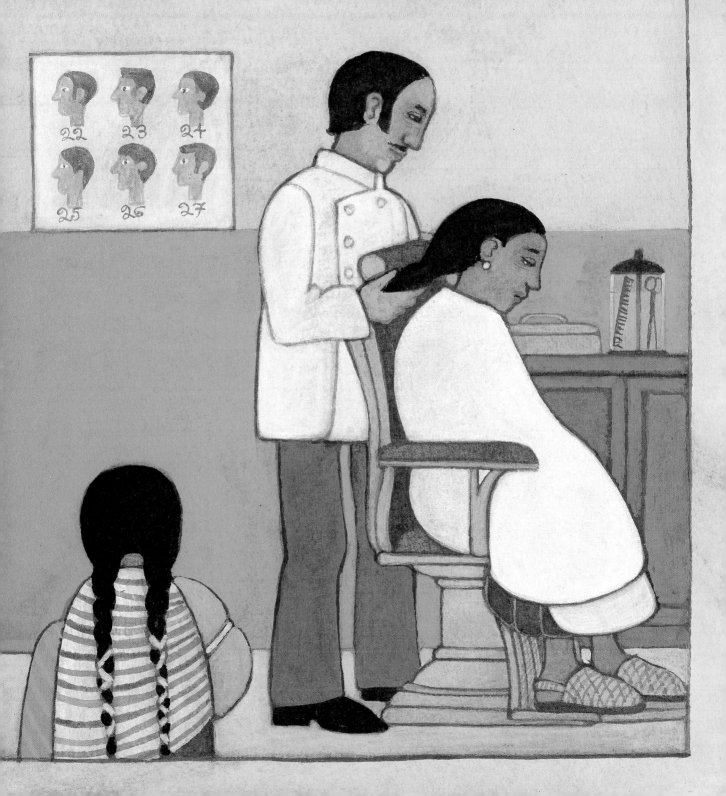

"Your hair is not long enough," she heard the barber say.
Her mamá's face reddened with embarrassment. Without a word, she got out of the chair and took Erandi's hand. As they turned to leave, the barber noticed Erandi's braids. "Wait," he called out. "We will buy your daughter's hair."

Mamá whirled around. "My daughter's hair is not for sale,"
she said proudly. Then she felt the pull of Erandi's hand and
looked down.

"*Sí*, Mamá, we will sell my braids," Erandi whispered.

"No, *mi hija*," Mamá said. "You don't have to sell your hair."

But Erandi let go of her hand and walked toward the chair.
The women stared as she climbed up onto the seat.

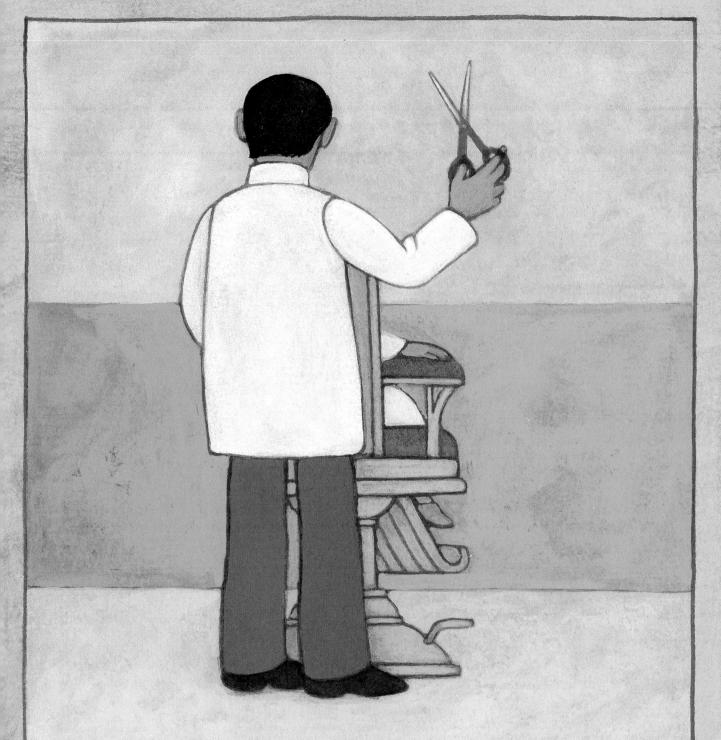

The barber measured her braids and picked up his scissors.
Erandi closed her eyes. Her hands turned cold when she felt the
metal scissors rub against her face and neck and she heard the
sharp *snip snip*.

The barber moved to the second braid and Erandi's eyes filled with tears. But she dared not cry. Instead she asked the barber, "Señor, will my hair grow back?"

"Of course! It will grow just as long and pretty as before," he told her.

Erandi kept her eyes shut until the barber had finished.
Then she opened them slowly and looked in the mirror.
Her hair reached just below the bottom of her ears.

Out in the street, the air was cold on the back of her neck. How strange it felt without her hair. Mamá walked beside her, not saying a word. Only the hollow clapping of their *huaraches* broke the silence of the cobblestone streets.

Why didn't Mamá speak? Was she angry with her for cutting her hair? Or maybe the haircutter had not paid enough for her braids?

Finally Erandi peeked at her mamá's face and saw she was crying. "Forgive me, Erandi, I shouldn't have let you sell your hair," Mamá sobbed, wiping her face with an old handkerchief.

Now Erandi understood that her mamá was not angry with her. She had only been thinking of Erandi's hair. "Don't worry, Mamá. My braids will grow back as long and pretty as before."

"Your hair was the longest and most beautiful of all," her mamá said.

Erandi paused for a moment, then asked shyly, "Mamá, did they pay you enough to buy a new net?"

"*¡Sí, mi hija!* They paid us more than I expected. We can buy a new net *and* the doll you wanted." She gave Erandi a big smile, and Erandi had never felt happier.

Then Mamá took Erandi's hand in hers, and as the last rays of sun lit up the rooftops, they turned and went back to the square to buy Erandi's doll.

# AUTHOR'S NOTE

In the nineteen forties and fifties, the use of women's hair for the production of wigs, eyelashes, and fine embroidery became increasingly popular in the country of México. Representatives from cosmetic and textile factories traveled into the state of Michoacán, searching for the unusually long, beautiful hair of the Tarascan women.

Every spring, merchants drove their vehicles through Pátzcuaro, the main Indian village. Their loudspeakers broke the silence of the quiet streets, inviting the local women to sell their hair.

A set of long, thick braids was the main source of feminine pride for the Tarascan women. The villagers believed that a stranger's scissors might cast an evil spell. Once the women sold their hair, they feared that it might become cursed and would never grow back. But financial hardship would often force them to sell it.

Today, the market for the purchase of women's hair no longer exists in the village of Pátzcuaro.